For Megan

First U.S. edition 2003

Library of Congress Cataloging-in-Publication Data
Sharkey, Niamh.
The ravenous beast / Niamh Sharkey — 1st U.S. ed.
p. cm.
Summary: Various creatures from a mouse to a whale describe all the things they can eat,
but the Ravenous Beast proves to be the hungriest of all.
ISBN 0-7636-2182-X
[1. Hunger — Fiction. 2. Animals — Fiction. 3. Monsters — Fiction.] I. Title.
PZ7.S52982 Rav 2003
[E] — dc21   2002035003

2 4 6 8 10 9 7 5 3 1

Printed in China

This book was typeset in Sharkey.
The illustrations were done in oil.

Candlewick Press
2067 Massachusetts Avenue
Cambridge, Massachusetts 02140

visit us at www.candlewick.com

The Ravenous Beast

Niamh Sharkey

CANDLEWICK PRESS
CAMBRIDGE, MASSACHUSETTS

"I AM

THE HUNGRIEST
ANIMAL OF ALL,"

said the Ravenous Beast.
"I'm hungry, hungry, hungry!
I'm so hungry I could eat
the big yellow house on the hill.

Gobble it up! Swallow it down!

Now THAT'S what I call hungry!"

"Nonsense! Smonsense!"

said the little white mouse.

"No one's hungrier than me.

I'm so hungry I could eat

a red boat and a ringing bell.

Nibble nibble! Tuck 'em away!

Now THAT'S what

I call hungry!"

"Hokum!
Pokum!"

said the marmalade cat.

"I'm as hungry as can be.

I'm so hungry I could eat

a bucket, a spade, and some pink lemonade.

Gnaw 'em! Gulp 'em! Stuff 'em down!

Now THAT'S what

I call hungry!"

"Hooey!
Phooey!"

said the spotted dog.

"No one's hungrier than me.

I'm so hungry I could eat

a roller skate, a birthday cake,

a rubber duck, and a ticking clock.

Slurp 'em! Burp 'em! Woof 'em down!

Now THAT'S what

I call hungry!"

"Moo! Moo! Malarkey!"
said the black-and-white cow.
"I'm as hungry as can be.
I'm so hungry I could eat
a castle, a crown, the Queen's dressing gown,
a rubber boot, and all the King's loot.

Munch 'em up! Crunch 'em down!

Now THAT'S what I call hungry!"

"Balderdash! Baloney!"

said the green crocodile.

"No one's hungrier than me.

I'm so hungry I could eat

a suitcase, a magic wand, a jack-in-the-box,

a polka-dot sock, a top hat, and a spinning top.

Snip 'em up! Snap 'em down!

Now THAT'S what I call

hungry!"

"Flip! Flap-doodle!"
said the grinning lion.
"I'm as hungry as can be.
I'm so hungry I could eat
a ray gun, a rocket,
a toffee from my pocket,
a trampoline, a trombone with a dent,
a bouncing ball, and a circus tent.

Bite 'em up! Bolt 'em down!
Now THAT'S
what I call
hungry!"

"Mumbo-jumbo!"

said the big-eared elephant.
"No one's hungrier than me.
I'm so hungry I could eat
an airplane, a parachute,
a pot of tea, a hot-air balloon,
a can of beans, a package, a kite, and a green bus.

Suck 'em up! Scoff 'em down!

Now THAT'S what
I call hungry!"

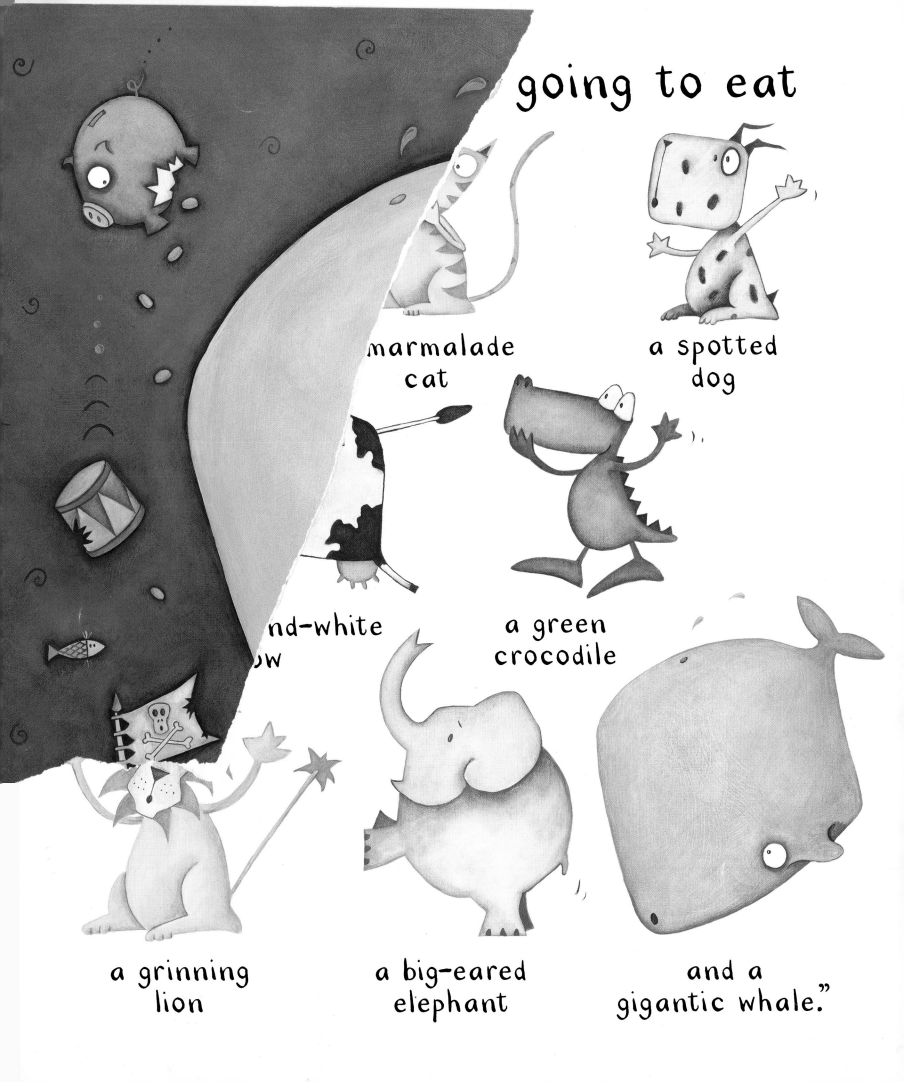

going to eat

marmalade
cat

a spotted
dog

nd-white
ow

a green
crocodile

a grinning
lion

a big-eared
elephant

and a
gigantic whale."

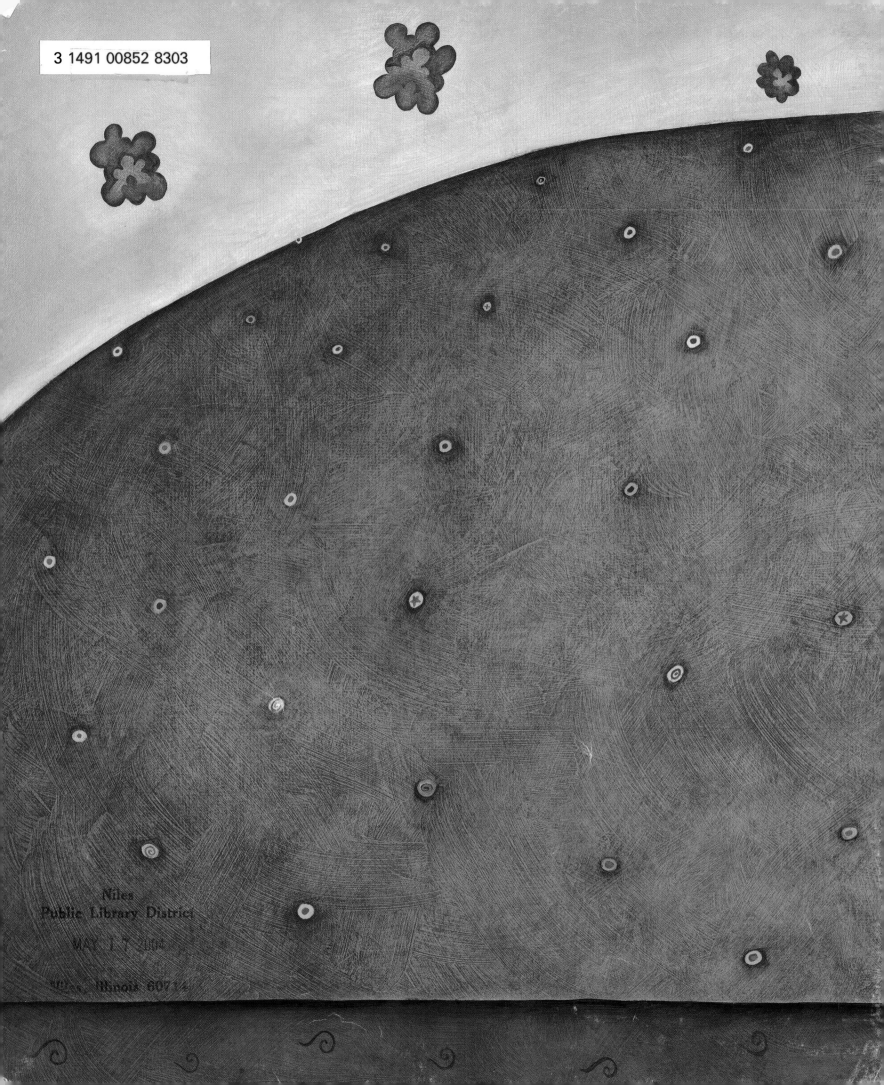